Contents

fiction Green

Brandon Robshaw

Published in association with
The Basic Skills Agency

Hodder & Stoughton

A MEMBER OF THE HODDER HEADLINE GROUP

Acknowledgements
Cover: Dave Smith
Illustrations: Stuart Williams

Orders: please contact Bookpoint Ltd, 130 Milton Park, Abingdon, Oxon OX14
4SB. Telephone: (44) 01235 827720, Fax: (44) 01235 400454. Lines are open from
9.00 - 6.00, Monday to Saturday, with a 24 hour message answering service.
Email address: orders@bookpoint.co.uk

British Library Cataloguing in Publication Data
A catalogue record for this book is available from The British Library

ISBN 0 340 84842 1

First published 2002
Impression number   10 9 8 7 6 5 4 3 2 1
Year   2005 2004 2003 2002

Typeset by SX Composing DTP, Rayleigh, Essex.
Printed in Great Britain for Hodder & Stoughton Educational, a division of
Hodder Headline Plc, 338 Euston Road, London NW1 3BH by Athenaeum
Press, Gateshead, Tyne & Wear.

1

A Day at the Beach

It was the first day of Mr Knox's holiday.
Every year, he went to the seaside
for two weeks.
He always went on his own.
He wasn't married
and he didn't have many friends.
He didn't mind.
He liked his own company.
He liked going for walks.
He liked looking round old churches
and local museums.
He liked sitting and looking at the sea.

On his first day, he went down to the beach
and sat in a deck chair.
He had a flask of tea with him
and a packet of sandwiches.
He sat and watched the waves.
He watched the people go by.
He ate his sandwiches.
He drank his tea.

Most people would call it a boring day.
Mr Knox didn't mind being a bit bored.
He liked a quiet life.
When he was younger,
he'd hoped for excitement,
but none ever came his way.
Now that he was middle-aged,
he liked a quiet life.
He was a strange man in some ways,
but a harmless, gentle man.

He watched the sun slip down in the sky.
Soon it would be evening.
It was getting quite cold.
He should be getting back to his hotel.
There was shepherd's pie
on the menu that night.
Mr Knox liked shepherd's pie.

He got up and gathered his things together.
As he walked off,
his foot hit something.
Something sticking out of the sand.
What was it?
Mr Knox bent down to look.

2

The Box

Mr Knox put his hand in the sand.
He felt something wooden and pointed.
Like a corner of something.
Mr Knox brushed the sand away
and tried to pull it up.

As soon as his fingers touched it,
something happened.
He felt a slight shock.
Like an electric shock.
He felt a tingling in his guts.
He was scared and excited –
he didn't know why.

At the same time,
the sun went behind a cloud.
It was suddenly dark.
A cold wind sprang up.

Mr Knox brushed more sand away.
He could see more of the thing now.
It looked like a wooden box.
His feeling of excitement grew.
He was breathing hard
and his heart was beating fast.

He pulled at it again.
At first, it wouldn't move.
Then it suddenly came free.

He held it in both hands and looked at it.
It felt strangely cold.
As if he had just pulled it out of a fridge.
There were carvings on the lid.

He blew the sand away.
He saw pictures of devils and demons.
They looked very real.
As if their deep-set little eyes
were really looking at him.
Their hands were stretched out
as if they were trying to grab him.
Whoever carved this
was a real artist, thought Mr Knox.
A master.
The carvings were brilliant –

and also a bit scary.

There was some strange writing
on the box, too.
Mr Knox couldn't read it.
It was in an alphabet he'd never seen before.
Some sort of ancient language.
Runes, or something.
For some reason,
he didn't like the look of them.
As he looked at them, he shivered.

He had a strong feeling
that he should bury the box again.
Hide it under the sand.
But he couldn't.
He felt too excited.
He had to see what was inside.

3

As Tight as a Clam

He tried to open the lid of the box.
It wouldn't open.
He pulled as hard as he could.
He tried to get his fingers under the lid.
The box was shut tight.

It must be locked.
There was no key, though.
There was no keyhole, either.
How were you supposed to open it?
He looked at the box again.
Again he felt the demons' eyes staring at him.
It must be very old, he thought.

Worth a lot of money.
He'd take it back to his hotel.
See if he could get it open there.
If not, he could always
take it to a museum.
An expert would know how to open it.

What if there was treasure inside?
It might make him rich.
That would change his life.
He could go on a world cruise.
At last, thought Mr Knox.
Something exciting has happened to me.

Then that feeling came back.
A feeling of fear.
He shivered again.
He felt as if he was being told to bury the box.

Go back to the hotel without it.
'I won't do it,' said Mr Knox out loud.
He didn't know who he was talking to.

He set off along the beach, carrying the box.
It seemed to get heavier and heavier
as he walked along.
He didn't understand
how it could be so heavy.

The wind grew stronger.
It was blowing right into his face,
trying to push him back.
It made an eerie howling noise.

It wasn't a pleasant walk back.
He was glad when he reached the hotel.

4

Major Wilson

When Mr Knox got back to the hotel
he went for a drink in the bar.
He felt worried and uneasy.
Perhaps a drink would raise his spirits.

Major Wilson was in the bar.
He was a retired army man.
He had come here for the golf.
He nodded to Mr Knox.
'Evening. What have you got there?'

'It's a box,' said Mr Knox.
He put it down on the table.

'I found it on the beach.
What do you think?'

Major Wilson looked at the box.
He didn't touch it.
'Very strange,' he said.
'Never seen writing like that before.
Don't like the carvings much.'

'I'm wondering what to do with it,'
said Mr Knox.
'I can't get it open.'

'I wouldn't try if I were you,'
said Major Wilson.
'I don't like the look of it.'

'Do you think I should take it to a museum?'

'If I were you, I'd take it back to the beach
where you found it,' said Major Wilson
'Leave it there.'

'Oh no, I can't do that,' said Mr Knox.
'I'm not doing that.'

'Well, that's my advice,' said Major Wilson.
'Take it or leave it.
I don't like the look of that thing.
It looks evil.
Got some sort of curse attached to it, I'd say.'

'Oh, I don't believe in
things like that,' said Mr Knox.
He finished his drink.
He picked up the box
and stood up.
'Well, goodnight.'

'I hope it is,' said Major Wilson.
'For your sake.'

5

Time for Bed

Mr Knox got into his pyjamas.
He took out his false teeth.
Then he sat on the edge of the bed
and picked up the box.

It still felt cold to the touch.
The faces of the devils and demons
seemed to be staring at him.
Again, he had the feeling
that they were reaching out to clutch him.
He shivered.
He could see what the Major meant
about the box.

It did have an evil feel about it.
As though it had some sort of curse attached.
Mr Knox pushed the thought aside.
He didn't believe in curses or evil spells.
That stuff was all nonsense.

Then, something very strange happened.
The box seemed to twist in his hands.
As if something in it had moved.
Something alive.
Of course that was nonsense.
All the same, the feeling was so strong
and so unpleasant that
Mr Knox put the box down.
He didn't want to touch it again.

He'd take it to a museum tomorrow
and let someone else deal with it.

He got into bed and turned out the light.
He felt worried and slightly sick.
As if he was waiting for
something unpleasant to happen.

The feeling kept him awake a long time.
He heard the clock strike twelve,
then one, then two.
Before it struck three,
he had drifted into a sleep of uneasy dreams.

6

A Bad Dream

Mr Knox dreamed he was back on the beach.
It was night-time.
The sea whispered.
Moonlight gleamed on the waves.

The box was at his feet.
He looked at the carved figures.
To his terror, he saw that they were moving.
They were pointing at him.
Coming towards him.
Their hands reached out for him.
Then, slowly, the lid begin to open.

His terror grew.
At the same time,
he had a burning curiosity
to see what was inside.

Now the box was half-open.
He thought he saw something dark
moving around inside.
His terror grew so great
that he had to scream.

He woke up with a jolt.
He sat bolt upright in bed.
He was covered in sweat.
His heart was going like a machine gun.

Calm down, he told himself.
It was just a dream.
He forced himself to breathe slowly.

He looked at his watch.
Half-past three.
Everything was quiet . . .
But no. No, it wasn't quiet.
He could hear a noise.
A sort of scratching noise.
It was coming from the box.

7

The Hand

Mr Knox got out of bed.
His terror was strong,
but his curiosity was stronger.

The box was on a table.
It looked bright silver in the moonlight.
The scratching noise
was clearly coming from inside.
As Mr Knox watched, the lid moved.
It didn't quite open.
It rattled.
As if something was pushing at it
from inside.

Mr Knox took a deep breath.

He reached out.

He took hold of the lid.

He pulled –

and the lid opened quickly and easily.

A hand shot out
and grabbed Mr Knox by the wrist.

8
'Help!'

For the second time that night,
Mr Knox screamed.

He tried to pull away
– but the grip of the hand was
much too strong.
It held him like a vice.

The hand was grey
and covered in long black hairs.
The sharp fingernails dug into his flesh.
Blood ran down his arm.

'Help!' he screamed.
'Help me!'

The door burst open.
Major Wilson rushed in.
'What the devil–?' he began.
Then he saw what was happening.

He rushed across
and tried to pull Mr Knox's wrist free.
But the hand's grip was far too strong.

'Ugh!' said Major Wilson.
'Foul thing!
Wait – I know what to do!'
He took a lighter from his
dressing-gown pocket.
He flicked it on.
He held the yellow flame
against the grey hand.

The smell of burning hair filled the room.
The hand wriggled, madly.
It let go of Mr Knox's wrist.

The Major slammed the box shut.
'We've got to get rid of this thing.'

'I couldn't agree more,' said Mr Knox.
Then he fainted.

9

Back to the Beach

First Major Wilson took off the cord
of his dressing-gown.
He wound it round and round the box.
He tied the tightest knot he could tie.
Then he wrapped it up in a carrier bag.

He brought Mr Knox round
by splashing cold water on his face.
'Come on,' he said.
'Show me where you found this thing.'

The two men left the hotel.
A howling wind blew
through the empty streets.

They walked until they reached the beach.
The tide was out.
The howling wind blew
even more angrily here.
'Where did you find it?' asked the Major.

'Round about here,' said Mr Knox.
'Just near these steps.'

The wind blew sand in their faces as they
dug a hole with bits of driftwood.
They dug deeper and deeper.
At last the hole was as deep as a man is tall.

'That should do it,' said Major Wilson.
He dropped the box in the hole.
They shovelled the sand back in the hole.
The wind dropped, and all was quiet.

Neither man spoke much
on the way back to the hotel.

10
The End of the Story

That's the end of the story, really.
Mr Knox never went back to the beach.
He'd had enough of beaches.
He never found out any more about the box.
He didn't want to.
The Major said there were a lot of strange
things in the world,
and mostly it was best to leave them alone.
Mr Knox agreed.

Mr Knox spent the rest of the holiday
peacefully enough.
He went for walks in the country.
He had tea in tea shops.

He looked round old churches.
By the end of the holiday,
he was more or less back to his normal self.

Not quite, though.
He still has five small scars on his wrist
where the hand's fingernails
dug into his flesh.
He is still very nervous about opening boxes.
And to this day,
he can't bear shaking hands with strangers.